I0692531

Francis Bennoch

**Sir Ralph de Rayne and Lilian Grey**

A legend of the Abbey Church, St. Albans

Francis Bennoch

**Sir Ralph de Rayne and Lilian Grey**
*A legend of the Abbey Church, St. Albans*

ISBN/EAN: 9783337086916

Printed in Europe, USA, Canada, Australia, Japan

Cover: Foto ©Andreas Hilbeck / pixelio.de

More available books at **www.hansebooks.com**

# SIR RALPH DE RAYNE

# AND LILIAN GREY

A Legend of the Abbey Church, St. Albans

By FRANCIS BENNOCH, F.S.A., M.R.S.L., ETC.

STRAHAN & CO., PUBLISHERS

56 LUDGATE HILL, LONDON

1872

LONDON:
PRINTED BY VIRTUE AND CO.,
CITY ROAD.

TO

# THE LORD HIGH PRESIDENT

AND OTHER MEMBERS

OF

## THE NOVIOMAGIAN BROTHERHOOD,*

This Legend is Dedicated

AS A REMEMBRANCE OF THEIR VISIT TO

ST. ALBANS,

JULY, 1869,

BY THEIR LAUREATE.


\* See Note 1.

# A LEGEND OF THE
# ABBEY CHURCH, ST. ALBANS.*

THE Summer sun shone brightly down,
And burnished MARTYR ALBAN's town,*
As, 'wakening from its drowsy state,
It rose for the approaching fête.

The clamorous bells in joyance rang,
The harpers harped, the minstrels sang,
Triumphal arches bared the trees,
Gay banners fluttered in the breeze,
As thronging through the narrow street
Came buoyant youths and maidens sweet,
And sprightly dames, and stolid squires,
And youngsters clad in gay attires;
For she, the fairest of the land,
Had pledged her troth, would give her hand

* See Notes 2 and 3.

To one right worthy, loved by all,—
SIR RALPH DE RAYNE, of VINTRY HALL:
And now had come the nuptial-day
Of brave SIR RALPH and LILIAN GREY.*

Bands trooped from GORHAMBURY'S towers,*
From old St. MICHAEL'S shady bowers,*
From ROYAL WINDSOR'S princely halls,
And HATFIELD'S ivy-mantled walls:
From SOPWELL'S cloisters, dark and low,*
Came hooded nuns in movement slow,
So prim, precise, demure, and staid,
They bring the brighter picture shade.
Think not they come to bless or cheer:
No! firm in purpose, proud, austere,—
Resolved to excommunicate
The gentle bride as renegate;
For she had come beneath their ban,
In listening to the vows of man
Against their creed, which blazoned stood
To guide the dreary sisterhood:
"The pure in heart should rise above
All passion throes of human love."

* See Notes 4, 5, and 6.

They seemed so gentle—void of art—
They almost won the maiden's heart;
And yet she could not help but feel
That something more than holy zeal—
Seclusion stern—a weary call!—
The GOD of life demands from all.

So wonder not the dismal train,
Emerging from the neighbouring plain,
Should seek the ABBEY CHURCH, and there*
Denounce the recreant sister fair.
Oh, what to them love, joy, or health !
They knew she had unbounded wealth,
Which, from the ages far away,
Concentred now in LILIAN GREY.
The loss of one might peril both,
Which made the pious sisters wroth—
Wrath keenly felt and undisguised :
Revenge was sweet—revenge they prized.

The curse a wandering monk had framed
The ABBESS as her own proclaimed.
Severe and cold, o'er her white face
No smile e'er crept with rippling grace,

* See Note 7.

Which, welling up, reveals the good
In kindly-hearted womanhood.
The lip compressed, the pallid cheek,
And deep-set eye, fell purpose speak.
To firmly seize and cast aside
All hindrances to power and pride.


Apart the Abbess musing stood,
Conflicting passions stirred her blood,
A hidden fire was seen to burn,
Some secret thought she seemed to spurn ;
In slow, deliberate undertone
She spoke—'twas well she stood alone :
" What if the maid my might defies ?
What if her lord my threats despise ?
I've that within my secret power
Will make the boldest blanch and cower.
Even at the altar, whilst they stand
Husband and wife, clasped hand in hand,
My voice shall rise—so loud and clear
That heaven, and earth, and hell may hear
Anathema!—that withering cry—
Go, sleepless live—unpardoned die !"

An orphan child, the maiden fair
Was left beneath the ABBESS' care,
To cherish, guide, and recreate,
In manner worthy her estate.
Though kept within the cloisters' gloom,
The early bud was now in bloom,
The cheek assumed a richer dye,
A deeper lustre filled the eye ;
With knowledge and experience grew
Impulsive yearnings, sweet and new—
A wider range, a deeper sense
Of woman's power and consequence ;
Her thoughts, matured, refined, profuse,
Were ne'er designed for hidden use.
The sisters sought her heart to gain—
" *Perhaps as* ABBESS *she might reign.*" ,
But ere her term novitiate closed,
SIR RALPH a different life proposed.
Unknown to abbess, nurse, or guard,
They met, where none kept watch or ward,
Beneath the shade of arching trees,
Whose leaves made music in the breeze.
A fitter place could not have been
For knight and maid to woo unseen.

How many a day from morn till eve
The dull routine her soul would grieve !
Or if relieved by menial toil,
Her spirit would from all recoil.
In contrast to her murky cell,
Where sickly odours dankly dwell,
Was that serene and lovely sight,
The starry sky and moon so bright :
Why, self-immured, there die and rot,
Forgetting all, by all forgot,
When she, like any bird, might be
Uncaged, a being blest and free ?

How sweet to feel his circling arm,
His pleasant breath, come soft and warm,
Or, looking up, believe his eyes
Were starry guides to Paradise !
The tale was told—the truth revealed,
And loving lips the compact sealed.

Tradition still with rapture swells,
As on the rare event it dwells,
On each minutest circumstance,
Of steed, and banneret, and lance ;

How, in their dazzling suits arrayed,
Shone those who joined the cavalcade,
And formed a bridal train so gay,
As body-guard to LILIAN GREY.


Two noble pages tripped beside,
To urge, restrain, or gently guide
Her prancing palfrey, creamy white,
With gorgeous trappings all bedight,
Perfect in form —with ambling tread,
And arched neck, and comely head,
With whinnying voice and ears elate,
As proud to bear so fair a freight.
O'er breezy fields they gaily moved,
Through winding lanes the blossoms loved,
Adown the sloping west they came,
Passed fields with poppies all aflame,
Skirting the miller's lake-like dam,*
Where swans in pride of plumage swam,
And over buried VERULAM !
Old HEATHEN VERULAM, whose stones*
Were filched to build the church, whence tones

* See Notes 8 and 9.

Of prayer and praise continuous rise,
In lifting spirits to the skies!
As our weak frames of dusty clay
Must toil and fret their little day,
With hope, and fear, and joy, and strife,
Preparing for a loftier life!

The bride alighted at the gate,
Where smiling dames her coming wait,
With swelling hearts and kindly eyes,
To greet the blushing sacrifice.
They quickly form a bridal train,
And up the aisle march twain and twain;
The matrons first, and then the bride,
Then rosy bride's-maids, side by side,
Who at the altar steps divide,
And stem awhile the flowing tide.

Three score of virgins, draped in white,
Bear baskets piled with blossoms bright,
To strew with flowers and leaflets rare
The pathway of the wedded pair;
Approach with measured step—defile,
And line with light the bending aisle:

Youths, smiling, watched the dainty feet
Keep time to music low and sweet.
So fair a sight had seldom been
In sacred fane or palace seen.

A mason carving high—alone—
The stately column's clustered stone,*
Suspended work, to watch below
The ceaseless current's ebb and flow ;
The graceful forms—the glistening eyes—
The whisperings sweet—the fond replies,
By which the cherished hope's revealed,
And hearts with love are touched and sealed.
He, musing, gazed until they seem
The mirror'd phantoms in a dream.
Transfixed he sate :—when all were gone
He felt insensible as stone ;
But never more resumed his skill—
The column stands unfinished still !

The church was filled above—below,
With ladies bright, a lovely show
Of rounded forms and radiant eyes,
Which sculptors might as models prize,—

* Notes 10 and 11.

When through the eager, waiting crowd
A whisper ran : " Behold a cloud,
Foreboding ill, inveils the sun !—
The hour-glass sand has nearly run !—
The bride awaits !—the bride's forgot !—
The laggard knight deserves her not ! "

Uncertain as the winds—they change ;
Now all rejoice, since HUBERT STRANGE,
From off the high embattled tower,
Descried the nearing cloud of stour :
" Within a mile their plumes appear—
Soon, soon the bridegroom will be here ! "

If others murmured, RALPH DE RAYNE
Might well of our neglect complain ;
To him and his, in sooth, 'tis time
We bend the current of our rhyme.

From ancient hall and bustling town,
From grassy vale and upland brown,
The noblest, bravest of the land,
To swell the bridegroom's joyous band
Came coursing up with dawning light,
To cheer the heart, and please the sight,

So full of frolic, youth, and glee,
The flower of England's Chivalry.

A score of miles, or more, divide
The happy bridegroom from his bride ;
And thus from VINTRY's fair abode
The gathered gallants early rode ;
They rode through forests deep and dark,
O'er furzy heaths, by grange and park,
Through narrow ways—o'er open plains,
With gorges ploughed by recent rains.
On, on they rode with songs of mirth,
Whilst Summer sunshine bathed the earth.
Though most were handsome, fair and tall,
SIR RALPH rode high—a head o'er all ;
In hawking, hunting, joust, or ring,
They were his subjects, he their king.
And when they reached the rounded
    height,
Whence ALBAN's CHURCH appeared in sight,*
With reverence bowed each faithful knight.
The lovely view that met their eyes,
Awakened wonder and surprise ;

* Note 2.

C

The undulating valley green,
The sombre woods, the glades serene,
The glittering VER, in windings bright,
Like thread of molten silver white,—
What more on earth could man of bliss
Desire than such a home as this?

A while entranced, they glad surveyed
The lovely scene of light and shade,
And half reluctant moved again,
Descending slowly to the plain.

Where two roads joined,—a dusky shade
By overhanging branches made,—
A moment's halt was called for, there
To set the train in order fair.

The word was given, again they move
Some paces on, beyond the grove,
Where stands the sculptured DRUID STONE.
Whence—why that shriek and heavy groan?
An arrow, shot from bow unseen,
Athwart the host, with glittering sheen,
Flew like a flickering bolt of light,
With point of steel and feather white,

And pierced the neck of RALPH DE RAYNE,*
Who prostrate fell upon the plain.
A quivering throb—a pool of gore—
In death he lay, to rise no more.

Alarmed, each knight his comrade scanned,
Each fearing each the deed had planned.
Whilst all, with consternation blind,
Stood still, the traitor slipped behind.
And quickly sprang the bank, and flew
For refuge in the Forest New.
It happed, that whilst he urged his horse
Through tangled ways of fern and gorse,
A knight who'd wandered from the throng,
A minstrel knight, who conn'd a song,—
A bridal song, of smiles and sighs,*
To win applause from ladies' eyes,—
Brave MONTE Rocco, from PROVENCE,
Who deftly plied sword, pen, and lance,
Was roused from his delicious dream,
When flashed across his eyes a gleam,
Reflected clear from polished steel.
He started—paused—with lifted heel

* See Note 12, and " Bridal Song," p. 29.

Stood high—beheld a cowering knight
Retreating from the troop in flight.
Suspecting cowardice, or wrong,
He thought no more of tune or song ;
Nor reasoned he—the impulse given
Seemed inspiration straight from heaven.
He clutched the rein—clipped close the knee,
For none his Arab steed could flee.
Resolved at once, he gave him chace—
'Twas pity few beheld the race !
With every bound of flying BESS,
The space between grew less and less ;
As nearer and more near he drew,
Too well the crouching knight he knew.
Swift as the lightning's scathing flash,
His glittering blade was drawn, and crash
Through casque of steel, of azure blue,
He clove the grizzly head in two :
As down the unerring falchion fell,
Up rose, released, a hideous yell,
In circles, eddying round and round,
Till swallowed by the yawning ground ;
The gibing laugh, the dying wail,
Made even MONTE ROCCO quail.

Recovering from his sense of dread,
He thus apostrophised the dead :—
" Oh, heaven is just, and will avenge ;
I now my sister's wrongs revenge !
'Tis thou, false ULRIC ! false as hell,
Near whom no innocence could dwell ;
A recreant knight—a Monk forsworn—
To rapine, lust, and murder born ;
Abjured of heaven, thou hast thy doom,
And hell might well deny thee room !
I thank the POWER SUPREME, DIVINE,
Thy work, accursed, is stayed by mine."

The spirit freed would homeward go,
The carcass fed the wolf and crow ;
The avenging knight recrossed the plain,
To join the weeping wedding train ;
A truer knight ne'er poised a lance,
Than MONTE Rocco, of PROVENCE.

Whilst noble hearts for vengeance burn,
Now to the Abbey Church we turn,
Where all in expectation wait :
The PRIEST in grand array of state,*

* See Note 13.

With crozier, crucifix, and hood,
Near the exalted altar stood,
To give his benedictive sign,
And make the civil bond Divine.

Why shrinks the bride ? why turns she pale ?
Why clings she to the altar rail ?
With eyes fixed on the iron grate,
Where great Duke Humphrey lies in state,*
Before her glistering, glaring eyes,
A shadowy form is seen to rise :
'Neath raiment, thin as woven dew,
A spectre form is beaming through,
With lifted hand and sunny smile,
Comes noiseless up the stony aisle.
Unchecked, through all, she sees it glide—
Now—now 'tis standing by her side ;
And oozing down from neck to chest,
A trickling crimson stains the vest !
She nothing feels, and yet can see
The form droop slowly to its knee ;
Her hand it gently raised, and pressed
With tender fondness to its breast,

* See Note 14.

And on her finger placed a ring,
Whilst faint seraphic voices sing
A strain that told of love and home,
The sweet refrain—" *Beloved, come!*"
Enrapt, she listen'd to the theme,
That seemed like music in a dream.
Another form she now beheld,
A form well known in days of eld,
With areoled brow—one hand outspread,
Which wreath-like rays effulgent shed,
That seemed to rest on either head.
His left hand held a feathery palm,*
His face out-beamed with heavenly calm.
'Twas HOLY ALBAN, from his throne
Come down, to bless them as his own,
And, blessing, faded from her sight
As clouds are melted into light.
In vain she strove to move or speak,
And aid from her betrothed would seek.
All dumb and motionless she stood,
Till glancing on the HOLY ROOD *
She turned—would speak to RALPH—but where
She thought he stood was empty air!

* See Notes 15, 16, and 17.

With clasped hands she stared with awe,
As she alone the vision saw.

The matrons start, with looks amazed,
Cry "Hartshorn! ho! the bride is crazed!"
As quick to help they all approach,
And on the altar steps encroach ;
When, with a calm beseeching eye,
An upturned look, a stifled sigh,
She raised her hand and whispered "Stay!"
Then bent as if she meant to pray.
A silence spread profound o'er all,
You might have heard a feather fall,
When, through the yielding air, so still,
Was heard a sweet faint voice, "I will!"
As died away the thrilling sound,
Fair LILIAN fainted to the ground.


Aghast, spectators held their breath,
"Can this be feigned, or is it death?"
They first recoiled, then forward crushed,
But in a moment all were hushed.
The mitred priest stooped down to see,
And raised the lady to his knee ;

Her lily temples gently pressed,
And placed his palm upon her breast :—
" Alas, alas! her days are o'er,
Fair LILIAN sleeps to wake no more! "

The joyous sounds that rode the gale,
Had now become a funeral wail ;
The cheeks that swelled with lusty cheers,
Were channelled now by streaming tears ;
As through the thinly peopled vale
Spread wide the strange and piteous tale;
Too soon 'twas known, SIR RALPH DE RAYNE
Had all unshrived been foully slain.
The instant brave SIR RALPH had died,
That moment sank his lovely bride ;
Though lost, yet found—to them 'twas given,
To wing as one their flight to heaven.

The minstrel's song was left unsung,
The curses wild were left unflung ;
The blossoms rare were left unstrewed.
Like statues there the maidens stood ;
One heavy, all-absorbing grief
Oppressed them, till they found relief

In sighs, and sobs, and scalding tears,
Which o'er their cheeks in glistening spheres
Rolled rapidly, and as they rolled,
Of sympathising anguish told.

Soon, soon within the transept's shade
A bier was raised—the bodies laid ;
Bells ring with muffled murmurs low,
The incense rises, candles glow ;
From fretted roof and cloisters dim *
Resounds the solemn requiem.†
How beautiful !—there, side by side,
His left arm pillowing his bride ;
Not clothed in robes of sable night,
But in their wedding raiment bright !
Death may divide—death here has wed,
The bier become their bridal bed !
No clouds by night shut out the stars,
No mist by day the sunshine mars ;
The cloudless sky, serene and deep,
Seems watching o'er them as they sleep.

With Sabbath dawning spread a cloud
Enshrouding all the sky ; a crowd

* See Note 18.          † See " Requiem," p. 31.

Of silent mourners came—each brow
With cypress wreath was circled now.
Within the chancel's solemn gloom
Was made a deep, a holy tomb;
Where gently were together laid
The brave young knight and lovely maid.
The entrance bore this legend—Pray
For Ralph de Rayne and Lilian Grey.


But ere their radiant forms were hid
From loving eyes by coffin lid,
The bride's-maids came, and pleading sought
The veil and wreath their hands had
    wrought, *
Should in the church suspended be,
That every coming age might see,
In those memorials fair, but frail,
The germs of this our touching tale.


And there the relics hang on high,
And Time's destroying touch defy;
For year by year young virgins strew
The church with flowers, the wreath renew.

* See Note 19.

So long as ALBAN'S CHURCH shall stand,
To tell its story to the land,
This legend ne'er shall pass away,
Of RALPH DE RAYNE AND LILIAN GREY.

# BRIDAL SONG.

### BY MONTE ROCCO.

MERRILY, merrily, ring the bells—*
  Ring the bells—ring the bells !
O'er hill and plain, the sweet refrain,
  In sounding joy, melodious swells.
      Ring the bells, ring the bells;
      Oh, merrily ring the bridal bells !

They come, they come, the vale along,
  Like morning beams the gentle bride ;
They come, they come, with lyre and song,
  The bridegroom moves with manly pride.
      Ring the bells, ring the bells;
      Oh, merrily ring the bridal bells !

Now—now the pealing organ sounds
  In cadence low, or loud and clear,
Till every heart with rapture bounds :
  Oh ! blessings are rained in music here.
      The organ swells, the organ swells,*
      How grandly now the organ swells !

* See Notes 20 and 21.

Again, oh ! merrily ring the bells,
　　Ring the bells, ring the bells !
The rite is done, the two are one,
　　Each heart with joy unbounded swells.
　　　　　　Ring the bells, ring the bells ;
　　　　　　Oh. merrily ring the marriage bells !

## REQUIEM.

ADOWN, adown, adown, in the deep dark tomb are
laid
Our brave young knight, our lady bright, the grave
their bridal bed.
The sun that rose so full of joy has set in misty
clouds ;
The bride who should a wife have been, the veil of
death enshrouds,
And by her side the bridegroom lies—all still his
manly voice.
There let them rest, for they are blest, and we may
well rejoice,
That brave young knight and lady bright should
peacefully be laid
Adown, adown; adown, adown—shower blossoms
on their bed.

Above, above, above, beyond the blue serene,
Our brave young knight, our lady bright, are with
the angels seen ;

Their robes of clay are cast away, and far beyond
the clouds
They wing their flight to realms of light which sor-
row never shrouds :
On ! side by side, beyond the tide, which life from
death divides,
As one they sing with seraphim where endless love
abides.
The spirits bright of maid and knight from
trouble are at rest,
Above, above ; above, above, in regions of the
blest.

# NOTES.

[The Author thanks Mrs. Nicholson, widow of Dr. Nicholson, so long the beloved Rector of the Abbey Church, for many useful hints, and would express his obligations to the friends who supplied other information.]

## Note 1.

THE Society of Noviomagus was founded in consequence of a small party of Fellows of the Society of Antiquaries having agreed to make an excavation at Holwood, near Keston, in Kent, on the spot which was supposed by Stillingfleet and other antiquaries to be the Roman station of Noviomagus, mentioned in the Itinerary of Antoninus.

About a quarter of a mile from the Roman works called "Cæsar's Camp" is a tumulus, known even at the present day as the "War bank," and here the party commenced operations. They discovered the foundations of a temple and several ancient stone coffins, Roman remains, &c. These were described in a paper read before the Society of Antiquaries on the 27th November, 1828, by Mr. Alfred J. Kempe,

D

followed by another paper by T. Crofton Croker. Mr. Balmanno and Mr. W. H. Brooke were also present.

After a meeting of the Society of Antiquaries on the 11th December, 1828, a small party interested in the matter adjourned to Cork Street, Burlington Gardens, and a society, "to be called the Society of Noviomagus," was then and there instituted. The following week, the same party being present, these were elected :—

| | |
|---|---|
| T. Crofton Croker . . | President. |
| A. J. Kempe . . . . | Vice-President. |
| Robert Lemon . . . | Treasurer. |
| H. Brandreth . . . | Poet Laureate. |
| W. H. Brooke . . . | Principal Artist in Ordinary. |
| Robert Balmanno . . | Secretary, *pro. tem.* |
| John Rouse . . . . | Usher of the Black Rod. |

Subsequently the following gentlemen were elected :—

| | |
|---|---|
| W. Jordan . . . . . | Father Confessor. |
| W. H. Rosser . . . . | Secretary. |
| J. Bowyer Nicholls . . | Typographer. |
| Rev. J. Lindsay . . . | Chamberlain. |
| Sir William Betham . | Genealogist. |
| J. R. Planché . . . . | Dramatist. |
| Thomas Saunders . . | Attorney-General. |
| W. J. Thoms, F.S.A. . | Notes and Queries. |
| William Wansey, F.S.A. | The Fishmonger. |
| F. W. Fairholt . . . | The Draughtsman. |

They met every Thursday evening, after leaving

Somerset House, at some convenient place in the neighbourhood, to partake of a supper, which, in those primitive days, consisted of Welsh rarebits, potatoes and butter, Glenlivat whisky, lemons, and sugar; and, at the close of the session, a trip was arranged to Keston Cross and other places of interest.

The present members are—

| | |
|---|---|
| The Lord High President | S. C. Hall, F.S.A. |
| The Baronet | Sir F. G. Moon, Bart., F.S.A. |
| The Architect | George Godwin, F.S.A. |
| The Physician | Dr. Stevenson, F.S.A. |
| The American Minister | Henry Stevens, F.S.A. |
| The Sculptor | Joseph Durham, F.S.A. |
| The ex-Sheriff | Charles Hill, F.S.A. |
| The Librarian | Joshua W. Butterworth, F.S.A. |
| The Photographer | Dr. Hugh Diamond, F.S.A. |
| The Friar | Edwin H. Lawrence, F.S.A. |
| The Absentee | Charles Ratcliffe, F.S.A. |
| The Associate | Wm. Chaffers, (late) F.S.A. |
| Treasurer, Laureate, and Acting Secretary | Francis Bennoch, F.S.A. |

Thirteen, the original number of members enrolled, continues a rule of the brotherhood.

### Note 2.

" MARTYR ALBAN'S TOWN;" also "ALBAN'S CHURCH."
(Pages 7 and 17.)

In respect of situation there are few abbeys in England superior to that of St. Albans, standing as it does, so grandly on the summit of a hill, surrounded by a large extent of richly varied and interesting landscape. On the other side of the Ver are the gentle slopes of ancient Verulam, and beyond and around are lovely heights covered with noble woods, producing effects of beauty and richness of effect probably unequalled. An old rhyme says—

> "When Verulam stood,
> St. Albans was a wood;
> Now Verulam's down,
> St. Albans is a town."

*Note 3.*

## ST. ALBANS AND VERULAM.

The finest view of St. Albans is obtained from the south side, on the raised ground, where, still in the ruins of the massy walls, may be traced the power of the Romans, the once mighty conquerors of the world, and the extent of the ancient and great city of Verulam, from which St. Alban went forth to the grassy slopes of the opposite hill, resolved and willing to die as the first British martyr to the faith in Christ. From this eminence, the site of ancient Verulam, the site is one of picturesque beauty. Where St. Alban shed his blood, rises in majestic grandeur the venerable Abbey Church, surrounded, or nearly so, by the modern town of St. Albans. The little river Ver, from which the ancient city took its name, meanders gracefully through the valley, until it joins the Colne, some four miles to the south-east. In the summer time, the fertile fields of waving corn, the green meadows, and the sylvan scenery, complete a picture which the mind cannot contemplate without pleasurable emotion.—*Mason*.

The Holy Alban was slain because he had sheltered, and allowed to escape, Amphibolous, a deacon of the Christian Church, and brought upon himself the death from which he had rescued his friend. Many churches were built, and dedicated to the name of the proto-martyr, notably St. Alban's, Wood Street, which was built by Offa, King of the Mercians, and used as his chapel, being contiguous to his palace in London.

*Note* 4.

LILIAN GREY.  (Page 8.)

Edmond, Earl of Kent, was originally Lord Grey of Ruthyn, and created Earl by Edward IV. He had a son, Sir Anthony Grey, whose mother was daughter of Henry Percy, Earl of Northumberland. It has been stated that he was killed at the battle of St. Albans; this, however, is doubted: some confusion having arisen between Grey of Ruthyn and Sir John Grey of Groby, killed in the battle, fighting on the side of Lancaster; and his widow, Elizabeth Woodville, became the Queen of Edward IV.—*Dr. Nicholson.*

The precise relationship of Lilian Grey to these noble houses it is difficult now to determine.

### Note 5.

GORHAMBURY AND ST. MICHAEL.   (Page 8.)

On the floor is the brass effigy of Rauff (Ralph) Rowlott, merchant of the Staple at Calais, an ancient company of foreign merchants, incorporated by Edward III.   He was the lineal ancestor of Sarah, Duchess of Marlborough.   The estates of Gorhambury and Sandridge, with others, had been granted to him by Henry VIII. at the dissolution of the monastery.   His son dying, his two daughters became co-heiresses.   Mary or Margery, the eldest, inherited Gorhambury, and married John Maynard, Esq., of Easting, in the county of Essex, who sold the whole of his estate in the neighbourhood of St. Albans to Sir Nicholas Bacon, Knight, afterwards Lord Keeper of the Great Seal in the reign of Queen Elizabeth.   Bacon was buried in St. Michael's Church.

The ancient Watling Street seems to have passed a little to the southward of St. Michael's Church, and led past Gorhambury, the residence of the Earl of Verulam, where a portion of the ruins of the mansion of Robert de Gorham, and where Lord Bacon resided, may still be seen.—*Dr. Nicholson.*

*Note 6.*

" FROM SOPWELL'S CLOISTERS." (Page 8.)

Matthew Paris relates that two women having entered on a recluse life in a hut which they had constructed near the river, the abbot built a house for their better accommodation, placing therein thirteen sisters under the rule of St. Benedict. As the first two women used to dip their dry bread in the water of a neighbouring spring, the place was called Sopwell.

Books were printed at St. Albans as early as the year 1480. The first treatise on hunting which ever issued from the press was the " Boke of Saint Alban," written by Dame Juliana Barns (otherwise Berners), the Prioress of Sopwell, and printed in the monastery, 1486, a copy of which is in the collection of Earl Spencer, and another in the University Library, Cambridge. It is divided into three sections : one on hunting, one on fishing, and one on coat armour—a curious study for a nun.—*Dr. Nicholson's History.*

*Note 7.*

"SHOULD SEEK THE ABBEY CHURCH." (Page 9.)

In 1077, Paul, of the Abbey of Caen, in Normandy, was appointed to preside over St. Albans, and within eleven years constructed the greater part of the Abbey Church. He was powerfully assisted by his kinsman Lanfranc, Archbishop of Canterbury, who was succeeded by Anselm, Abbot of Bec. The new church was magnificently dedicated on the 5th of the Kalends of January, 1115, by Geoffrey, Archbishop of Rouen, assisted by Robert, Bishop of Lincoln, Roger of Sarum, Ralph of Durham, and Richard of London, and many more abbots, in the presence of King Henry I., Matilda his Queen, and many earls, barons, nobles —illustrious personages of whom the number is unknown because of the multitude, on which day all remained feasting and rejoicing in the Court of St. Alban, the blessed Protomartyr of the English. —*Buckler's History,* p. 5, &c.

## Note 8.

### "Miller's lake-like dam." (Page 13.)

"Many buildings in the occupation of the Abbey stood in its immediate vicinity : the Grange and the Mill were ranged towards the west and extended over a considerable surface, and large tracts of land, including the orchards, pasturage, and fish-pools stretched along the southern side, supplying by their various stores the constant demands of hospitality, contributing in no small degree to the character and splendour of the domain."—*Buckler's History*, p. 166.

## Note 9.

### "Old heathen Verulam, whose stones." (Page 13.)

Matthew Paris expressly records the fact that the ruins of Verulam were resorted to for supplying materials for the re-edification of the church. The evidence seems irresistible that the material was not made for the Church of St. Albans, but that the building was to some extent designed to suit the materials. The bricks and tiles were doubtless formed eight centuries before the time when they were used to construct a Christian church, and may have been taken from the theatre or the temple of the gods. From the foundation to the uppermost courses of the walls, even to the parapet of the tower, is of tile construction. Verulam, with the addition of some portions of the old Saxon church, which was wholly destroyed, served to construct the new building of the Abbey Church.

The bricks were very large, measuring $16 \times 12 \times 1\frac{1}{2}$; and one discovered on the site of Verulam, and preserved at Oaklands, weighs 21 lbs.—*Condensed from Buckler's History*, p. 22, &c.

### *Note* 10.

#### " THE STATELY COLUMN." (Page 15.)

The most remarkable instance of attempting to harmonise the different periods of architecture occurs in the eighth pillar from the west end on the north side of the nave. The broad members in the front, and in one reveal, have been formed with segments of circles, and the intermediate angles sloped off—a rude resemblance of the clustered columns opposite, and at the west end—but the attempt was not sufficiently encouraging to be persisted in, and the mutilated column remains, as it was left, unfinished by the workmen.—*Buckler's History*, p. 144.

*Note* 11.

## " THE STATELY COLUMN'S CLUSTERED STONE."
## (Page 15.)

" Here we observe the Norman or Romanesque style of the twelfth century, the Early English or first Gothic style of the thirteenth century, and the Decorated style of the fourteenth century. The place on the north series of arches, where the Norman ends and the Gothic begins, deserves notice. The clustered Early English pillars of the sixth arch of the nave spring *out of* the massive Norman pier."—*Mason*.

*Note* 12.

## "AND PIERCED THE NECK OF RALPH DE RAYNE."
## (Page 19.)

The first battle of St. Albans was fought on the 23rd May, 1455, between Henry VI. and Richard, Duke of York. A strong party, led by the Earl of Warwick, burst into the town with great shouting, and overcame the royal army, which lost heart and fled. The king, finding himself alone, and deserted, *and wounded in the neck by an arrow*, took refuge in a small cottage occupied by a baker, where he was found by the Duke of York, who with all courtesy conducted the crest-fallen monarch, first to the Abbey, and next day to London.—*Mason.*

*Note* 13.

" THE PRIEST IN GRAND ARRAY OF STATE." (Page 21.)

In the British Museum there is a picture headed " The Parliament holden at Westminster the fourth of Feb., the third yeare of our Sovereigne Lord King Henry the 8th, A.D. 1572," during the rule of Abbot Ramayge, in which the figure and dress of each ecclesiastic dignitary are depicted : abbots of least note lead the procession two and two first, and then those of higher dignity—the Abbot of Tewkesbury and the Prior of Coventry leading, and the Abbots of St. Albans and Westminster are the last pair.

All the abbots, with two exceptions, have the same dress—a plain cassock and cap with an ample robe of purple, having folds behind as a hood. None of the abbots wear mitres. The bishops wear the same simple caps as the abbots, and only the archbishops, who close the procession, wear the mitre.—*Nicholson.*

Robert de Gorham was the first abbot on whom

the mitre was conferred, and the Abbots of St. Albans were authorised by the Pope to take precedence of all others in England.—*Mason's Guide.*

### Note 14.

"WHERE GREAT DUKE HUMPHREY LIES IN STATE."
(Page 22.)

Humphrey, Duke of Gloucester, who died at Bury, Feb. 28th, 1447, was buried in the Church of St. Albans, where a superb monument was erected to his memory. He was fourth and youngest son of Henry IV., and Protector of the Kingdom during the minority of his nephew, Henry VI.

The iron grating is generally considered to be of a date prior to the erection of the monument, and was intended to give to pilgrims and other visitors in the aisle a view of the shrine in the centre of the Feretory, or Saint's Chapel.

Duke Humphrey founded the Divinity School at Oxford, and commenced the collection of books which formed the nucleus of the Bodleian Library; though all, save two, of the books presented by him were destroyed by the Visitors in the time of Edward VI.

The story of his death—murder rather—at Bury

St. Edmunds, and the details of the removal of his body to St. Albans, were published by the Camden Society, in 1856.

### Note 15.

#### "His LEFT HAND HELD A FEATHERY PALM."
#### (Page 23.)

On the 5th December, 1539, the king's commissioners came to St. Albans, when the fortieth abbot, Richard Boreman, *alias* De Stevenache, signed a creed of surrender, and delivered up the seal of the monastery, which is now in the British Museum. It is made of ivory, and represents St. Alban holding in his hand a branch of the palm-tree.—*Mason.*

### Note 16.

#### SHRINE. (Page 23.)

"Abbot Geoffrey, in the fifth year of his prelacy, commenced a glorious shrine of marvellous workmanship for the Blessed Alban, our patron. . . . . And he made it of hammered work raised and brought out, and he filled in the hollows with cement, and completed the elegance of the whole body of the shrine by a steeply raised ridge, and this still further beautified the whole.

" And when all the parts of the shrine were thus handsomely executed, he had the whole richly gilt, so that they rather appeared to be of gold than silver. From the ancient treasury of the church jewels were brought forth for its decoration—one sardonyx being of such size that it could scarcely be held in one hand, and none other was like unto it. This unrivalled stone was given to the church by King Etheldred, the father of Edward, the most pious king of England. All being prepared, the remains of the Holy Alban were duly translated thereunto on the anniversary of the festival of St. Peter."—*Condensed from Buckler's History*, p. 48, &c.

## *Note* 17.

" TILL GLANCING ON THE HOLY ROOD." (Page 23.)

" In the time of Abbot William of Trumpington, Master Walter de Colchester, then Sacrist, an incomparable painter and sculptor, erected a loft or *pulpitum* in the middle of the church, with its great Rood and Mary and John, and other carvings and handsome decorations, at the cost of the Sacristy, but by the diligence of his own labour.

" The altar was solemnly dedicated by John, Bishop of Ardfert, in honour of the Holy Cross, and the same bishop consecrated the great Rood, which, with its images, was placed over this altar. From which it is evident that an altar in honour of the Holy Cross, enclosed by an iron screen, stood at the entrance to the Sanctuary."—*Buckler's History*, p. 70.

### Note 18.

## "FROM FRETTED ROOF AND CLOISTERS DIM."
### (Page 26.)

Abbot Robert, in the twelfth century, erected one cloister along the east side. Abbot Trumpington constructed several others, chiefly of oak timber, some of which remain. Abbot Roger, who so greatly adorned the interior of the church, built a cloister against the south wall of the nave, in a superb style of architecture. The unrivalled elegance of the design baffles any attempt at description, and the hand which performed the work with such extraordinary delicacy and beauty had attained its utmost skill. But nothing now remains of this work than that which could not easily be severed from the wall of the church.—*Condensed from Buckler's History*, p. 258.

*Note* 19.

" THE VEIL AND WREATH," ETC. (Page 27.)

In the south aisle of the nave hangs the framework of a chaplet, and the tradition has been handed down, that it formed a part of a marriage garland of a bride, who died on her wedding day, and was said to have been buried near the spot.— *Mason*.

(If considerable liberty has been taken with dates, the unities of the poem may plead an excuse ; and I learn, with pleasure, that a niece of Dr. Nicholson has supplied the new wreaths for many years past).

*Note* 20.

" RING THE BELLS." (Page 29.)

" The Abbot Paul furnished the tower with bells, and a certain noble named Litholf, who resided in a woodland part of the neighbourhood, added one still larger and more laudable than the rest. Having a good stock of sheep and goats, he sold many of them and bought a bell, of which, as he heard the new sound when suspended in the tower, he said jocosely, ' Hark ! how sweetly my goats and my sheep bleat.' His wife procured another bell for

E

the same place, and the two together produced the most sweet harmony, which, when the lady heard, she said : 'I do not think this union is wanting of the Divine favour, which united me to my husband in lawful matrimony and the bond of mutual affection.' "—*Buckler's History.*

### Note 21.

### "THE ORGAN SWELLS." (Page 29.)

John of Wheathampstead was re-elected Abbot in 1451, and about this time gave to his church a pair of organs, on which and their erection he spent fifty pounds.

No organ in any monastery in England was comparable to one of these for size, and tone, and workmanship.—*Dr. Nicholson.*

### THE END.

PRINTED BY VIRTUE AND CO. CITY ROAD, LONDON.

# New Books and New Editions.

## The Library Edition of the Works of
ALFRED TENNYSON, D.C.L., Poet-Laureate. Vols. I., II., III., and IV. Post 8vo, 10s. 6d. each.

*.* This Edition will be completed in Five Volumes, to be issued at intervals of one month.

## Notes on England.
By H. TAINE, D.C.L., Oxon, &c. Translated by W. F. RAE, with an Introduction by the Translator. Reprinted, with Additions, from the "Daily News." Post 8vo, 7s. 6d.

## Character Sketches.
By NORMAN MACLEOD, D.D. With Illustrations. Post 8vo, 10s. 6d.

## Town Geology.
By the Rev. CHARLES KINGSLEY. Crown 8vo, 5s.

## Pansies.
"—— for Thoughts." By ADELINE T. WHITNEY. Square 8vo, 2s. 6d.

## The Days of Jezebel.
An Historical Drama. By PETER BAYNE, M.A. Crown 8vo, 6s.

## Tennyson's Songs :
Being a Collection of Songs and Ballads from the Published Works of ALFRED TENNYSON, D.C.L., Poet-Laureate. Square 8vo, cloth extra, 5s.

## Saint Abe and his Seven Wives.
A Tale of Salt Lake City. Crown 8vo, 5s.

STRAHAN & CO., 56, LUDGATE HILL, LONDON.

# New Books and New Editions.

—

## The Secret History of the International
By ONSLOW YORKE. Crown 8vo, 2s.

## Music and Morals.
By the Rev. H. R. HAWEIS. Post 8vo, 12s.

## Twilight Hours.
A Legacy of Verse. By SARAH WILLIAMS (SADIE) Third and Enlarged Edition. Crown 8vo, 5s.

## The Drama of Kings.
By ROBERT BUCHANAN. Post 8vo, 12s.

## Lord Bantam.
By the Author of "Ginx's Baby." Crown 8vo, 5s.

## Passages from the French and Italian
Note-Books of Nathaniel Hawthorne. 2 vols., post 8vo, 24s.

## Flowers and Gardens.
Notes on Plant Beauty. By FORBES WATSON, M.R.C.S. Crown 8vo, 5s.

## Peasant Life in the North.
Second Series. Post 8vo, 9s.

## Faust.
A Tragedy by JOHANN WOLFGANG VON GOETHE. Translated in the Original Metres by BAYARD TAYLOR. 2 vols., post 8vo, 28s.

———

STRAHAN & CO., 56, LUDGATE HILL, LONDON.